BEDTiME
for Sweet Creatures

words by **Nikki Grimes**

pictures by **Elizabeth Zunon**

sourcebooks jabberwocky

For Imani Lia and her own sweet creature,
Oghenebrume Naomi Anigboro.
—NG

To Mila. May your imagination run wild!
—EZ

Text © 2020 by Nikki Grimes
Illustrations © 2020 by Elizabeth Zunon
Cover and internal design © 2020 by Sourcebooks

Sourcebooks and the colophon are registered trademarks of Sourcebooks.

The full color art was created using oil and acrylic paint with cut paper collage, marker, and gel pen.

Published by Sourcebooks Jabberwocky, an imprint of Sourcebooks Kids
P.O. Box 4410, Naperville, Illinois 60567-4410
(630) 961-3900
sourcebookskids.com

Library of Congress Cataloging-in-Publication data is on file with the publisher.

Source of Production: Phoenix Color, Hagerstown, Maryland, USA
Date of Production: December 2019
Run Number: 5017658

Printed and bound in the United States of America.
PHC 10 9 8 7 6 5 4 3

You beat

the word

like a drum

the minute

I say,

"Come, sweet creature. It's bedtime."

Your eyes swell, wide as OWLS.
"Let's go," I say.

"who?

WHO?"

"BEaR is going," I say. "He'll be awfully lonely without you."

Suddenly,
you
come
running.

In the forest of your room, you cling to Bear.

I turn back the sheets, and you

GROWL.

"In you both go," I say.

You toss your **mane** and **roar**,
order me to check beneath the bed.

I kneel on the forest floor,
find something wild and ferocious.

"Meow."

Your bookshelf is **NOISY** with stories.

"Which one?" I ask.

You point, frozen

like a **FAWN**

until you hear

"ONCE UPON a TIME."

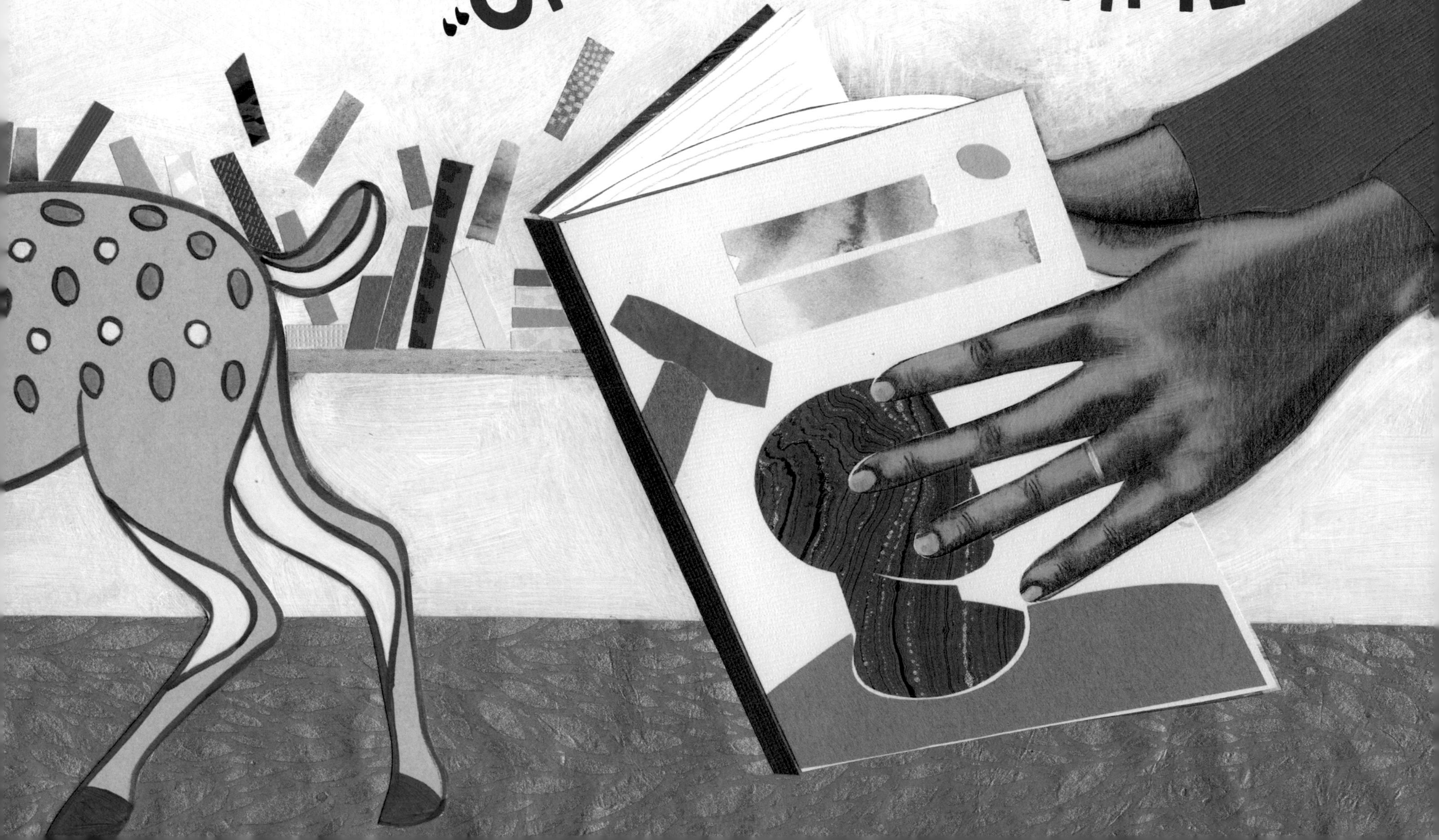

You yawn
and grind
your teeth like a
SQUiRREL,

ready to nibble the night.

"I'm
not sleepy,"
you tell me.

I smile and
tuck you in tight.

A **Koala**,
you hang
onto me
for
**one
last
kiss.**

"I **love** you,
mommy!"

"I LOVE YOU MORE."

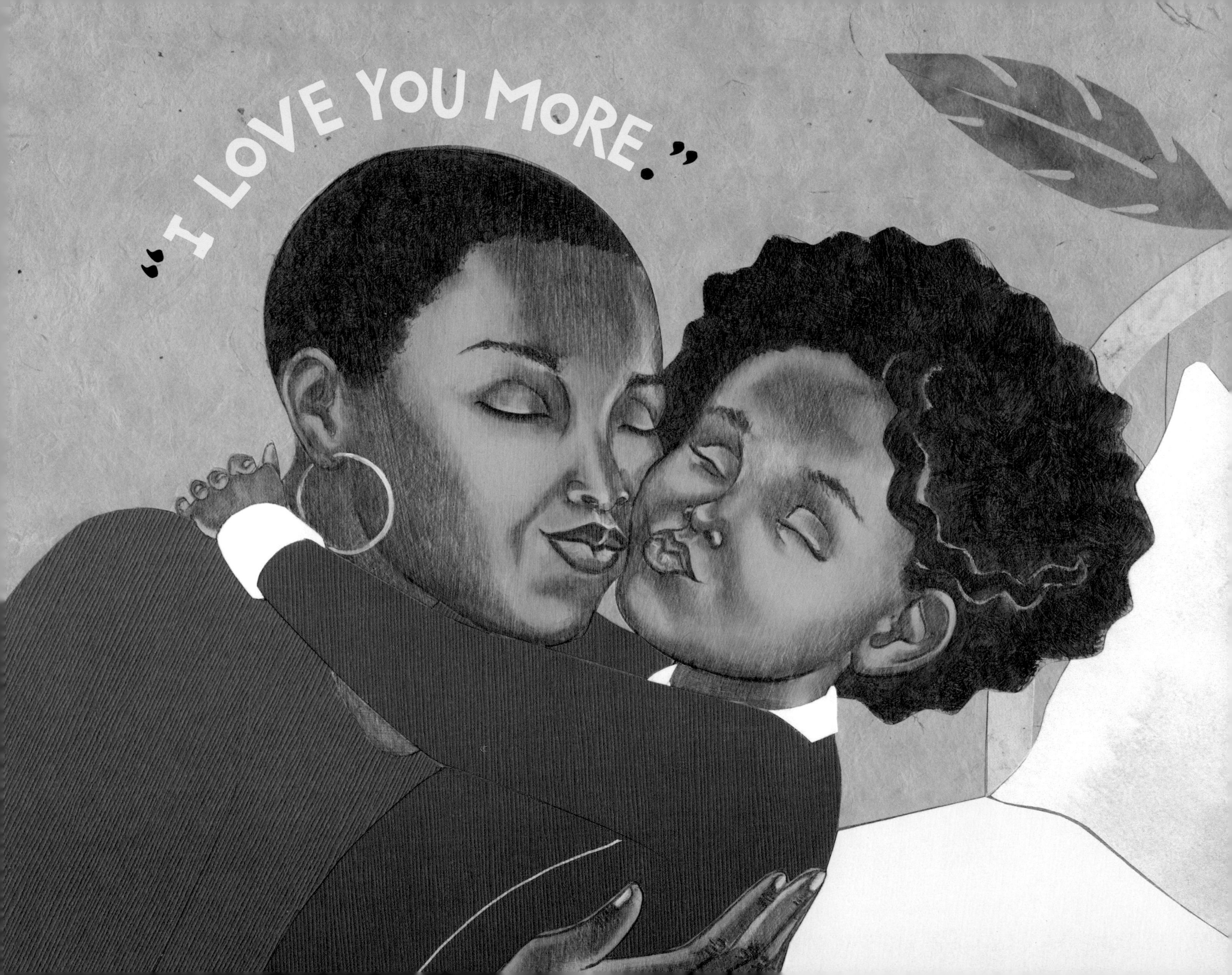

"OK. Lights out," I say.

Fearless **TIGER**, you crouch, just in case, ready to pounce on goblins in the dark.

Later, you bound out of bed,

SLY
WOLF

on

the

hunt

for

water.